The Vampire's Kiss

KENZIE SKYE

One

Brenna

What am I even doing here anyway? This is crazy. I pull at the hem of my little black dress, feeling completely out of place.

Of course, I suppose I *am* out of place. I'm in a huge ballroom full of vampires. There are some other humans here too, but they are few and far between.

I scowl when I feel the hem of my dress lift back up to mid-thigh. I don't know why I'm even trying. The fabric is just going to pull back up. It's not like I can stretch it down any farther.

Olga, my bestie, helped me get dressed for

this occasion, and I know she was right that I couldn't just show up here wearing my typical ripped jeans and tank top, but I'm feeling like such a fish out of water in these ridiculous clothes.

Olga brushed my long, wavy, dark hair out until it shines. I catch a glimpse of myself in one of the many mirrors lining the ballroom, and I have to grudgingly admit that I do look pretty—something I never really thought of myself as since I've always been more of a tomboy. I wasn't the girl who played with dolls as a child. Instead, I was the girl getting into fights with the boys and climbing trees.

And yeah, don't even ask me why they have so many mirrors in this vampire's castle. It's kind of weird seeing all the vampires passing in front of it and having no reflection, but hey, I guess they just like the opulent look of them.

And all these mirrors certainly make my task easier. I can easily discern if someone is a vampire or not by seeing if their reflection shows up.

Of course, it's pretty easy to pick vampires out anyway based on their appearance alone. Most of them have pale skin and almost blood-red lips, and of course they have that look of near-constant hunger in their eyes.

But for what I have in mind, it's better to be safe than sorry.

I don't want to waste this kiss on a mere human.

At least I don't have to worry about running into any werewolves here. The vampires and the werewolves don't get along very well.

Still, I don't much savvy the thought of kissing a vampire, but I'm so eager to come into my power that I can get over the thought of anything. Even kissing one of these deadly bloodsuckers.

I feel a flutter of excitement in my belly when I wonder what my power will be like. Oh, it's not like I plan on doing anything nefarious with my power either. It's just if I have some untapped source of power, I would like to have access to it. Plain and simple.

It'd be nice to use it to help with some of the chores around my house. It'd be nice to have it for protection when I'm walking down the city streets alone. Simple things like that. That's what I plan on using it for. I won't be looking to alter the course of the universe or anything.

How did I find out I have to kiss a vampire to unlock this untapped potential? Well, last Halloween when Olga and I attended one of those carnivals, we stopped by the fortune teller's tent, and I usually don't put much stock in those things, but what she predicted for Olga has already come true, so I'm revisiting her prophecy that said I have to kiss a vampire to unlock my hidden potential.

Hey, it doesn't hurt to try, right?

I never would have thought I was one of those humans who would have hidden powers within me. Of course. I never knew my parents. I've been an orphan for as long as I can remember. I'm not even sure how they died or anything.

I grew up at the local orphanage until I became friends with Olga in school. Then, her parents so kindly adopted me and made me the sister she always wanted.

Yeah, they're really great people, and I love them as if they were my real parents. I don't go so far as to call them Mom or Dad, though, because I was a little too old for all that whenever they adopted me in.

But still, they're my chosen family, if not by blood.

Christ, this is like something out of the Victorian ages. They're not playing modern hip-hop music. Instead, the gentle strains of a violin quartet—a live one at that—floats throughout the crowded ballroom.

Of course, I suppose this is more of the vampire's speed since many of them were grand-fathered in from the Victorian era.

My eyes scan the room. While most of them aren't wearing Victorian clothing, there are a few who are turned out in full Victorian dress. Most of the men are wearing modern suits and the women modern dresses, though.

I continue to scan the vicinity, glancing in the mirrors to double check potential candidates for a kiss. I have to pick my target and soon because it's nearing midnight.

I suppose I could just walk up to any random stranger and lay one on him, but I purposefully chose tonight—New Year's Eve—to do this because it's considered a little more socially acceptable to kiss a stranger on this night.

When the clock strikes midnight, almost everyone is willing to receive that New Year's Eve kiss for good luck, even if it is with a stranger.

I chew on my lip thoughtfully. There are so many choices. I don't even know where to begin.

It's not like I'm looking for the hottest or sexiest vampire. On the contrary, I'm looking for one who looks relatively unthreatening. I don't want one who's going to rip my throat out for my impudence. At the same time, a shiver of disgust passes through me when my eyes light on some of the older gentlemen with balding heads. They might be more agreeable to getting a random kiss from a random young woman, but I'm just not sure I can stomach that.

My eyes finally light on one who's not too young but not too old. He's probably in his late twenties, and he looks unthreatening enough. Not too handsome, yet not too hideous either. He's like the perfect medium, and I decide that he's probably my safest bet.

It's not quite midnight yet, but it's getting closer, so I start making my way toward him through the crowd. I'm not going to get too close to him. I don't even need to talk to him or anything. I just want to be near enough to him so that as soon as the clock strikes midnight I can jump out and quickly lay one on him. I'll make it quick and then be on my merry way.

Easy peasy.

Yeah, I think that's the best course of action.

My cheeks are flaming at the thought of kissing this random stranger, but I have to do this. If there's any slight possibility that there's truth to the fortune teller's prophecy I have to find out.

I square my shoulders and continue pushing through the throng of people until I'm hovering near him, trying to look as nonchalant as possible as the clock ticks down closer to midnight.

When there's only three minutes until the clock strikes, I begin nudging my way closer to him. One minute.

My palms get sweaty with nervous anticipation.

The countdown is beginning to start, and I don't see any other women around him.

My heart rate ticks up in my chest as the countdown gets closer to zero.

Ten.

Nine.

Eight.

Seven.

Six.

Five.

Four.
Three.
I inhale a deep breath.
Two.
One.
Here goes nothing.

Two

Jasper

My eyes narrow as my gaze hones in on the pretty little raven who stumbled into this ballroom looking completely out of place. She didn't come with anyone. She's here all alone, and that instantly sets my instincts on alert.

I've been around long enough to know that most pretty young females don't go to balls unescorted by male companions—or at least another female companion.

No, this little bird is up to something, and I'm going to find out what.

I've been watching her. She keeps casting

surreptitious glances all around the ballroom, almost as if she's looking for someone.

She keeps inching closer and closer toward the little circle of men over in the corner of the ballroom.

I know those men. They're the intellectual sort of vampires. The ones who think they're a cut above the rest. They still try to hang on to their humanity and sequester themselves off from the rest of us riffraff, which begs the question of why they're even here to begin with.

My lip curls up into a slight snarl as I look at them. Then, my eyes flip back over to the pretty little woman. She's a tiny thing. She keeps pulling at the hem of that damn dress like she's uncomfortable in it.

The fucker is way too short for my taste. Oh, she looks beautiful in it, no doubt, but I do miss the days of old when women wore dresses that completely covered their legs. That way every man's eyes didn't get to see what belonged to one man.

Her long, dark hair is a deep chocolate brown. It's almost so dark that it looks black, but not quite. Her eyes are a beautiful sapphire blue, and those lips are like rubies.

Of course, I know that they're stained that color from the red lipstick she's undoubtedly wearing, but I can't help marveling at how beautiful the contrast is against her creamy white skin.

If I didn't know any better, I would say she's a vampiress. She certainly has that look about her, but I can smell her blood thrumming beneath her vibrantly alive skin all the way over here. Plus, I see her reflection in the mirrors Garrington has ostentatiously placed all over this fucking ballroom.

I don't know what it is about the little raven, but I can't take my eyes off her. I'm drawn inexplicably to her—so much so that were she not a human I would believe that she's my mate. I feel a pang in my chest at the thought. Very few vampires have mates, someone who's meant to be solely theirs. I've spent centuries wandering this earth alone, hoping that maybe fate would be kind enough to give me one.

Even though I've never found my mate, I feel like I have one deep down in my soul. It's like there's another half of me that's missing.

My eyes drag down over the tiny human. Why do I feel like something is clicking into place inside me when I look at her?

But that can't be right because she's a human, and my mate has to be a vampire. I mean, that's just the way it is. Vampires don't have mates with other kinds, especially those of the living variety.

I frown as she keeps creeping closer to that group of men in the corner. The intellectual, snobbish pricks.

Does she know one of them? Is one of them someone she has a crush on?

The instant jealousy that flares within my chest at that thought surprises the hell out of me. I've never in all my centuries felt this kind of jealousy. The thought of this woman desiring another man fills me with an infernal rage unlike anything I've ever known. My nostrils flare, and I blink at the unexpected emotion.

I lift my glass of brandy up to my lips to take a thoughtful sip as I contemplate these foreign feelings.

Hey, just because we vampires mostly drink blood doesn't mean we can't enjoy a good cognac or brandy from time to time. What's more is the effects of alcohol don't affect us near as strongly. It takes me ten times as much alcohol to get as wasted as a human. And that's perfectly fine with me because while I like to enjoy a drink from time to time, I don't want to get shit-faced. Being inebriated only spells trouble. I like to keep my wits about me.

Another thing...I haven't noticed the tiny human take a drink at all, and that's probably because she looks way too young to legally drink. If I had to guess, I'd put her around eighteen. Barely legal.

I don't know how old I truly am, but my physical appearance stopped aging around the age of thirty. For centuries, I've looked like a man in his prime, and I suppose I am. Still, even physically, I look too old for such a sweet, young creature.

But fuck, everything within me is calling to her. Why is my hand closing into a fist around my glass the closer she creeps to Donovan?

I figured out who her sights are set on, and it's the nerdy-looking vampire with the smart-looking glasses and slicked-back hair. I eye him sardonically. What could she possibly see in him? He's not really what most women would call handsome. Of course, he's not hideous either. I know the fucker, though, and he doesn't have a charming bone in his body.

My eyes glance back at my little raven, the

questions churning in my mind. What's her story? Who is she? What does she want with Donovan?

I hear the countdown start, and I keep my eyes trained on her little form. She looks nervous, and I see her hands shaking against her dress even from over here. I frown.

When the countdown gets down to the count of ten, I see her take in a deep breath.

She begins moving toward Donovan, and then it suddenly dawns on me what's going on here, and I don't know why, but I'm fucking furious about it.

There is no way in hell I'm going to let this pretty little angel press her lips against his.

I move without thinking.

I'm in front of her in a flash, pushing Donovan back until *I'm* the one standing right in front of her.

Her eyes are closed, the dark lashes fanning over her porcelain cheeks as she stands on her tiptoes with her lips slightly puckered.

I'm like a moth drawn to the flame because I can't stop myself.

I close the rest of the distance between us and press my lips firmly against hers.

She gasps at the sudden contact, her mouth opening the slightest bit, and I take full advantage, slipping my tongue within her sweet depths.

And holy hell.

She tastes like sweet, pulsing life and honey.

I spear my hands into the long tresses of her hair as I angle her head back and plunder deeper into her sweetness.

I don't know who this tiny little human is, but she tastes like *mine*.

And I decide right then and there that I'm going to keep her.

Three

Brenna

God, who knew the unassuming-looking vampire could kiss like this?

I feel myself melting against him despite myself. My hands come up to catch myself from falling and press against a hard chest just as a strong arm wraps around me and pulls me flush against a body that's made of granite.

His mouth continues to plunder mine skillfully, his tongue sweeping in and out, flicking at my lips and twining my tongue with his.

I'm only supposed to be kissing him to unlock my powers, but I'm finding that I'm enjoying this kiss way more than I ever thought I could.

What's wrong with me? How can I enjoy a kiss with a vampire? This is crazy.

I let out a squeal of surprise when I realize how buff the chest under my palms feels.

That's funny. The vampire I had my sights set on didn't look nearly as big as this chest feels.

I open my eyes and stumble back with a gasp when I see the huge, hulking vampire in front of me.

This is not the one I had intended to kiss.

And just where had he come from? How did I end up missing my mark so completely?

I have to crane my head way back to look up at this vampire. He towers over me, and he's built more like a werewolf with his tall, alpha-looking form. It's obvious that he's ripped underneath that suit. I can practically see the bulging muscles straining against the fabric.

He has that pale complexion with dark hair that's stylishly disheveled. It's not swept back like so many of the vampires wear their hair. It's more like a beautiful chaos.

Fuck, he looks like one of those men who

you would see on the cover of magazines, a model.

I can't believe I just kissed someone this freaking gorgeous.

I shake my head as if to clear it, my thoughts turning back to my goal.

Oh my god, I just kissed a vampire. So now what do I do? Do I just wait? Are my powers supposed to be activated instantaneously?

Shouldn't this be more monumental than this?

I chance a glance up at the vampire who's looking down at me with burning eyes.

They were blue a moment ago, but now they're a beautiful golden color. They're shining down at me intensely.

I press my hand to my forehead absently. I can't think with him staring at me like that. Plus, my cheeks are flaming at the thought of what he thinks of me pressing my lips against him like this.

I need to get out of here. I need room to think and to see what's going to happen to me.

I spin on my heel and turn to hurry away from him. My mission is accomplished. Now I need to just get out of here and maybe find Olga and then wait for whatever is supposed to happen. Surely, something is going to happen, isn't it? I can't help the sharp prick of disappointment that bites at me when I consider the very real possibility that there's nothing to this prophecy, that I don't have any powers after all.

I haven't even made it out of the foyer before the insanely hot vampire is suddenly standing before me again.

I stop and stumble back at his sudden appearance.

I really hate how vampires can move in a flash like that.

"Where do you think you're going, little bird?" he asks me, his voice dark and sensual.

I feel my heart pitter patter in my chest as I look up at his big form. He's intimidating to be sure, but I've never been one to back down from a challenge, so I lift my chin bravely and tell him defiantly, "I don't really think that's any of your business."

His lips tilt up into a half grin. "Oh, I think it's definitely my business. When you kiss someone like that, little bird, you can't just fly away like nothing happened."

My cheeks redden further—if that's even

possible—as I sputter up at him, "That...that was a mistake. I mean...that kiss wasn't meant for you."

His eyes darken at my words, and his face pulls down into a frown.

"I'm aware." His voice is like ice. "It was for Donovan." He nearly spits the name before he lifts his own chin. "Who is he to you?" His jaw sets angrily.

I blink, surprised by his sudden anger. And who is Donovan?

"Who?" I ask. Is Donovan the name of the vampire who I'd really been trying to kiss?

He studies me for a moment as he rubs his forefinger and thumb over his chin thoughtfully. "You didn't know who he was, so why were you out there trying to kiss a random vampire?"

He takes a step toward me.

I take a step back.

"Again, that's not really any of your—" I start to say, but he cuts me off, moving like lightning to grab me and pull me flush against his chest.

I gasp as I crane my head back to look up at him. I feel his entire body pressed against mine, and while I might not have much experience with men, I know that hard thing pressing against my stomach isn't a gun.

Good lord, this insanely hot vampire is turned on—for *me*.

"It most certainly is my business," he states firmly, his eyes glittering down at me dangerously. I feel like I'm in the snare of a wild animal. One wrong move, and he'll bite me—literally.

I don't know what's going on here, but the way this vampire is holding me so possessively like he thinks I'm his or something has me feeling a little lightheaded.

"I don't even know who you are," I stammer.

"Jasper," he answers immediately. "And who are you, my little bird?" he asks as he trails a finger along the side of my cheek, studying me intently.

My breath hitches in my throat at the way he calls me his little bird.

"Brenna," I answer him before I can stop myself. Then, I mentally curse myself for giving him my name.

"Brenna," he repeats my name, and the way he says it sends a shiver up my spine. He feels it too if the way his eyes flare with heat are any indication.

"Well, pretty little Brenna, what were you

doing trying to kiss Donovan if you don't even know who he is?" His jaw clenches again.

I start to tell him, but then I catch myself and shake my head as if to pull myself out of the daze he seems to have put me under. I push against his chest, trying to break free from his hold, but it's to no avail. I won't be getting away from this vampire unless he chooses to release me.

"Let me go," I insist, not liking the feeling of being trapped.

"Not until you answer my question." He's holding me stubbornly.

I glare up at him. I really don't want to tell him anything, but it's obvious he's not going to let me go until I do, so I finally huff out, "It was a prophecy. I was told something would happen if I kissed a vampire."

Jasper's eyebrows shoot up into his hairline, but he keeps his face impassive as he asks me, "What was supposed to happen?"

I fight against him again, not wanting to share all this with him, especially since nothing has happened, and I feel like a complete idiot.

And I don't think I'll be able to bear it if he laughs at me. I'm already feeling stupid and embarrassed enough.

"It doesn't matter because it didn't happen," I spit at him.

He runs a hand along the side of my cheek and down through my hair when I continue to struggle, as if I'm a spirited mare that he's soothing. And as much as I hate to admit it, I do soothe under his touch.

I glare up at him again, resenting him for his ability to soothe me. "There? Are you happy? Will you let me go now?"

"What was supposed to happen, little bird?"

I feel my cheeks flaming again as I realize he's not going to let this go.

"I was supposed to come into my power," I tell him, my voice dejected.

He studies me for a long moment. I prepare myself for his ridicule, but it never comes. Instead, he studies me thoughtfully.

"What kind of power?" he finally asks.

I scowl at him. "I don't know, and it doesn't matter anyway. Didn't you hear what I said? Nothing has happened, so it was obviously a false prophecy." My shoulders slump with defeat.

I had been so hopeful that I had some sort of untapped power within me, something to validate me and make me special.

"I heard what you said, little bird," he answers me, "but it's not true."

I raise my eyebrows at him. Does he know something I don't? "What do you mean?"

"Something did happen." He licks his lips as he looks back down at me.

"You became *mine*."

Four

Jasper

I knew it. I knew the moment my lips met hers that she's my mate. Hell, I think I knew it even all the way across the ballroom. That's why I was so drawn to her. It doesn't make any sense because she's a human, but it is what it is.

One part of the legend that doesn't lie is that when you kiss your mate, you will know, and boy do I know. I felt that shifting within me. It's like she's suddenly a part of me and I've known her my whole life.

It doesn't even matter what her name is. It doesn't matter why she was trying to kiss a random vampire. This happened the way it was supposed to happen, and I don't know what she's talking about, unleashing some hidden power, but *this*, this is what was supposed to happen.

She was supposed to kiss me and become mine. *Mine*. My mouth salivates at just the thought. I want to taste her so badly. No, I won't drain her of all her blood and turn her into a vampiress, though my heart wrenches at the thought of her going through a human's natural transition of life and dying.

I push that thought out of my mind, though. We've got plenty of time for me to pitch the pros of turning into a vampiress to her because I have absolutely no intention of letting my mate die now that I've found her.

I've never heard of a vampire having a human mate, but we'll deal with this together. It's my assumption that the human must be turned into a vampire. Otherwise, how will we be together forever?

If she dies, she'll leave me. My chest clenches painfully at just the thought of being without her now that I've finally found her.

"Let me go," her little voice trills out. She's

struggling against me again, and I frown down at her.

Of course, while *I* may realize she's my mate, *she* obviously doesn't, and it's going to take some convincing.

That's fine. I have all the time in the world. Literally.

But there's no way in hell I'm letting her go.

"Never," I tell her, my voice serious. I mean it too. I'm never letting her go. I've spent too many centuries looking for her.

I wrap my arms around her and gather her close to me as I travel to my place. In the blink of an eye, we're standing in my library.

There, that's better. I already feel a satisfying calm seeing her in my place where she belongs. With me.

She stumbles, and I hold her arms to steady her.

Yes, a vampire's mode of travel is a bit over-whelming for humans at first.

She looks around with wide eyes. "What? Where are we? How did you—?" She continues to sputter, looking completely adorable in her confusion.

"You didn't know vampires could travel like so?" I ask her, amusement in my voice.

She shakes her head silently, still looking dazed.

"We're in my home. Our home," I clarify.

Her eyes go wide, and her mouth falls open into a little "o" as she looks up at me incredulously. She finally shakes her head, those pretty tresses bouncing with the movement, and crosses her little arms over her chest.

She lets out an incredulous laugh. "You're completely insane," she tells me.

I shrug, completely undeterred by her assumption. "Maybe."

"Look, Jasper," she begins, speaking to me slowly, as if I'm some sort of beast that she can charm. A thrill goes through me at hearing my name on her lips. I want to hear her panting it as I give her more pleasure than she's ever known. My cock stiffens at the thought, and I have to fight back a groan.

"You have to let me go. I'm not yours. Whatever you feel or think you feel, it's just an illusion." Her eyes are wide and pleading.

I chuckle. She really is completely adorable. Oh, she's preciously naïve if she thinks she's going to talk me out of this or that she has the type of wisdom that I have. I've been alive for centuries whereas she's been alive for...

"How old are you?" I suddenly ask her.

She blinks at the abruptness of my question before she answers, "Eighteen."

Christ, she's just a babe barely out of the cradle—especially compared to me.

So young. So sweet. So innocent. Why does that make me want to defile her even more?

"In all my centuries of roaming this earth, I've been looking for one thing," I tell her as I stalk toward her. "You."

Her eyes are wary, and she takes a step back from me.

I'm having none of that, though. I'm before her in a flash, causing her to gasp and fall back again, but I catch her in my arms and clutch her to my chest.

"Don't tell me you don't feel this connection between us," I rasp against her lips, my passion overcoming me before I claim those sweet lips once again. And God, she's just as sweet as before. I growl into her mouth as I deepen the kiss, unable to help myself.

I feel myself lengthening in my pants. Fire

like I've never known courses through my veins, hot and pulsing.

I kiss her deeply like a starving man, and I suppose I am. I've been starving for centuries, thirsting for her, hungering for her.

I trail my kisses along the side of her jaw, pausing when I reach the tender flesh of her neck. I can almost see her heartbeat there. I can certainly hear it, feel it.

She tenses underneath me, no doubt wondering if I'm going to bite her.

It takes every ounce of willpower I have in me to pull back. As much as I'm dying to taste her, I know that now's not the time, so I'll wait.

I'll wait until she's more comfortable with me. I don't want our first mating to be with her fearing me.

With great effort, I pull back from her and note the tremble in her frame, the flush to her countenance, the little puffy pants of her breath, the way her chest is moving up and down rapidly as if she can't suck in enough air.

Oh yes, she definitely feels it too, try as she might to deny it.

I drop my forehead to hers and breathe out

an admission. "Fuck, how you do tempt me, little bird."

She takes in a shaky breath before she hits me with another plea. "Please let me go. This is all a mistake."

I frown as I stroke my hands through the silky tresses of her hair. I can't stop touching her. I can't get enough of her. And I'm tired of hearing her call us a mistake.

"This is not a mistake," I tell her simply. "We're meant to be, and I'm not letting you out of my sight ever again."

This is non-negotiable. I will not release her. While I don't want her to resent me, I'm not going to chance losing her. Not now that I've finally found her.

She lets out a little huff before she changes tactics. "Okay, so maybe we are meant to be or whatever, but you can let me go. Let me go home, and then we can keep seeing each other. We can date or whatever you want," she proposes hopefully.

I let out on amused chuckle. I see right through her, of course. Does she honestly think she can trick me?

"Oh, little bird, you are precious," I tell her as I rub my thumb along her puffy bottom lip.

I watch the hope dim from her eyes and her shoulders deflate when she realizes her little tactic didn't work.

I try to ignore the pang her disappointment causes me, telling myself that she'll adjust to me in time.

"Let me show you to your room," I offer.

Even though I'm dying to, I won't claim her tonight. My little bird needs time to get used to all of this, so I'll give it to her.

But make no mistake. She is mine, and I will be taking her soon.

Five

Brenna

I'm cursing myself for ever believing in that stupid fucking prophecy. I've gone from a hopeful girl wanting to come into her non-existent power to the captive of an insane, possessive, obsessive vampire.

And captive is certainly what I am because Jasper keeps me locked up in this room. Oh, he visits me every day—multiple times a day—to spend time with me.

He tries to engage me in conversation. He kisses me. He skirts little touches all over me, but he doesn't push me for more—as much as I can tell he wants to. That tent in the front of his pants doesn't lie. I know he desires me, but he's not going to force me, and for that at least I am grateful.

I'd be lying if I said that his touches and kisses don't bring me a certain amount of pleasure.

The vampire is obviously a very skilled lover. For some reason, I feel a prickle of jealousy within me at the thought that he's been with other women. Because I mean, you don't live to be as old as he is without having some sexual experience.

But then it just pisses me off that I even feel a prickle of jealousy because he's nothing to me. He's my kidnapper, my captor, and I refuse to allow myself to fall for him, despite his insane notions that were fated to be or some shit.

I've got to get out of here. The only problem is I have no clue how to do that.

It's not even worth it to try to run from him because he can move in the flash of an eye. There's no way I can outrun him, so what I'm going to have to do is outsmart him.

"Why the dour countenance, my little bird?" he asks me as he strokes his hand through my hair.

He's always petting me like I'm a favorite pet or a little kitten. I grudgingly have to admit that it feels good to feel his fingers stroking through my hair. Of course, I'll never tell him that, though.

"I'm bored of sitting in this room day in and day out. Will you please let me go outside, Jasper?"

He blinks at my use of his name. I studiously refrain from saying it because I know how much pleasure it gives him. For some reason he likes to hear me saying his name. It's probably some sort of Neanderthal fetish of his.

He studies me thoughtfully for a moment before he finally speaks. "We can take a walk out on the grounds if you would like. There are several roses in bloom right now."

I reward him with my most genuine smile. "That sounds lovely!"

He looks surprised by my amicable nature. I'm usually surly as hell to him and pout the entire time he's around me, so I'm hoping he won't see through my guise. Hopefully, he'll just think that I'm starting to accept my situation here and am trying to make the best of it.

I don't really know how I plan on getting away from him when we get outside—only that I have to try. Running is out, so the only other thing I can think of is to somehow harm him, but how in the hell am I going to harm a centuries-old vampire who's stronger than an ox?

I'm contemplative as he selects a coat for me from the wardrobe he had stocked. Yes, Jasper thought of everything. He had a closet full of clothing that looks like it's hand-tailored just for me brought in. Every piece of it fits me like a glove, and I have to admit that these clothes are way more beautiful than anything I've ever worn in my entire life. Yet somehow he made sure they're just as comfortable as they are beautiful.

He holds the sleeves of the coat out for me, and I allow him to slip it onto my arms. He buttons me up, pushing my hands away when I try to do it on my own.

My heart trips within me. He has this little way about him. He likes doing things for me, taking care of me. It's completely frustrating yet endearingly sweet at the same time, and that's just the thing. That's part of why I have to get out of here—and quick. Because the longer I'm here, the more I'm softening toward him, and I'm sure that's his entire goal.

He hooks my arm through his and begins leading me out of the castle and into the gardens just like we're some sort of medieval couple, a suitor strolling me along on a mid-afternoon walk.

I don't fight it. I'm just grateful that at least I'm going to see the sunlight. Yes, that's one myth that is totally untrue. Vampires do not burn or die in sunshine. Jasper has absolutely no qualms about being in the sunlight, although he told me that he does prefer darkness since it's not as hard on his eyes, so the thought that he's putting his eyes through this discomfort for me also makes my chest flutter a bit.

I press my lips into a thin line as I firmly remind myself that I shouldn't feel any sort of pity for him. This is all his fault. He's kidnapped me. He's keeping me here against my will. I have to remember that.

But really, this is all your fault, another little

voice whispers in my head. *None of this would have ever happened if you hadn't been stupid enough to believe that prophecy and forced a kiss upon a vampire.* But how was I supposed to know that the prophecy was false and that I would get unlucky enough to kiss the most obsessive, possessive, insane vampire on the planet?

As we stroll along through the gardens, I can't help marveling at the beauty of his roses. He has roses of many varieties all curling up beautifully on the grounds. There are deep red roses, vibrant purple roses, lavender roses, soft yellow roses, coral roses, blush roses, and hybrids with white centers and pink tips. There's even a black rose.

"They're all so stunning," I marvel aloud as I finger their delicate petals and inhale their heady fragrance.

"Yes, beautiful," I hear Jasper murmur, but when I look up, he's looking at me—not the roses.

My heard does a little flip, and I feel myself blushing.

He expertly plucks one of the deepest red roses and places it behind my ear. He's careful to make sure no thorns prick my skin, and then it suddenly hits me.

Thorns. Vampires can be hurt with thorns. They're not exactly the same as a wooden stake. It won't kill him, but it should maim him long enough for me to get away from him.

My heart starts beating rapidly in my chest as I consider my options. I feel a prick of conscience at thought of hurting him, though.

But it won't kill him, I assure myself, *and you have to do what you have to do to escape.*

By all means, I suppose I should want him dead, but I can't bear the thought of completely destroying him. He hasn't been abusive to me. He's just kidnaped me.

Even I know how fucked up that train of thought is.

I bend over to admire one of the black roses. "May I?" I ask him.

He raises an eyebrow at me and cocks his head down in assent.

I pluck one of the black roses from the bush, making sure to break the stem so that there are plenty of thorns still left on it. I stand and start walking slowly over to him with the rose gripped in my hands covering the thorns. I feel the thorns pricking slightly against the skin of my palms, though not enough to draw blood.

I make my way over to Jasper and give him a tiny smile. His eyes are glittering down at me possessively, and my breath catches, both at his look and what I plan on doing. Why is my heart twisting within me?

I lift the rose up as if to place it in his lapel. I try to calm my nerves, but my arm shakes as the rose gets closer and closer to him.

Go on. Just punch it into him. You can do it. I mentally pep myself up.

My fingers are trembling so badly that I almost drop the rose. I take in a deep breath and pull back, getting ready to plunge the stem into his chest.

But then I suddenly feel Jasper's big hands surrounding mine.

I look up at him with dread and see the fire blazing in his eyes. His mouth is pressed into a thin line.

He tsks down at me. "Ah, little bird, you're going to have to be way smarter than that."

Oh god, he knows what I was up to.

He exerts just the slightest amount of pressure on my hands, but it's enough to cause me to lose my grip on the rose.

It falls to the ground between us ominously. Jasper stomps on it, his eyes dark as he suddenly yanks me against his chest and wraps his arms around me, teleporting us back to my prison.

Shit. What have I done?

Six

Jasper

I can't stop the pain that tears through me at the realization that Brenna was really going to stick me with a thorn bush. True, it wouldn't have killed me, but did she know that? And even if she did know, the fact that she would hurt me like that...

It's really no matter. I'd be healed in less than twenty-four hours, but it's the principle of the matter. I would never harm a hair on her head, but she would do that to me. She's that desperate to get away from me.

More so than the thought that she would hurt me physically is the realization that she abhors me that much. The irony of it is not lost on me. I have a mate who wants nothing to do with me.

I've been patient and kind and as indulgent of her as I can be all things considered. Every day, it takes every ounce of control I have to not claim her. It's killing me being so near her and denying myself. I have a perpetual case of blue balls because I wanted to give her time to want me of her own accord.

And this is how she repays me.

It takes more control than it took for me to not kill everyone in sight and drink every amount of blood I could find when I was a freshly changed vampire to keep from taking her innocence every time I'm around her. That's how hard it is to fight this when every instinct inside of me is screaming at me to make her mine in every way.

I'm suddenly tired of being patient with her. I'm tired of being the good guy. Hell, I'm a vampire. I'm a villain, a monster, and it's obvious that's all she'll ever see me as, so I might as well live up to my name.

She's going to be my mate whether she likes it or not.

My mind is trying to reason with me, telling me that she hesitated. I saw the tremble in her hands. I felt her fear. I knew something was up the moment she wanted to pluck the rose.

The knowledge still stings, though. My heart is hurt because I'm completely and irrevocably in love with this little human, my little bird, my little Brenna.

And I know that she desires me physically as well whether she'll admit it or not. I feel the way her heartbeat ticks up whenever I touch her. I feel the shiver that passes through her at my touch, the way she trembles in my arms.

It's time to claim what's mine.

She must see the intent on my face because she tries to apologize. "Jasper, I'm so sorry." Her voice is quaking as she tries to step away from me. "I didn't mean it. I wouldn't have done it."

I silence her by smashing my lips down on hers, kissing her deeply, possessively. This kiss isn't tender like so many of mine have been since I brought her here. I'm not trying to coax her.

No, this kiss is that of a monster unleashed. This is the kiss of a man who's at the end of his rope. It's a kiss of fire and passion, of frustration and anger.

As she always does, she melts against me, her body going limp in my arms. I wrap my arms around her triumphantly, holding her up so she doesn't fall to the floor at my feet, though my cock gives a little jerk at the thought of her on her knees in front of me.

"Lie to me! Lie to me and tell me you don't want this, little bird," I rasp against her lips, daring her to deny it.

She swallows and shakes her head.

"Say it!" I growl at her. "I want to hear the words. I want to hear you reject me again."

She looks up at me and presses her lips together, the look in her eyes torn. She wants to say it, but she can't, and damn if that doesn't make my cock a fucking rod of steel in my pants.

I knew it. She wants this. It's her mind that's fighting against her. She's probably telling herself all the reasons why this can't work—chief among them being that I'm a vampire and I've kidnapped her. She's painted me as the villain in her mind, but I don't really give a fuck now because this connection we have goes deeper than that, and I know once I get inside her she'll see that.

"Exactly, Brenna, you can't say it because you know it's true."

She opens her mouth, but no sound comes out, and I can't resist. With a groan, I kiss her again, delving my tongue into her hot heat as I begin to hump her sweet little mound through our clothing. I'm losing control. My hands are shaking, and the friction of my cock against her even through our clothing is enough to drive me mad with lust.

I've never expressly asked her before, but I already know she's a virgin. Virgins have a certain smell to their blood. The smell drives vampires crazy, and it's only amplified a thousand fold since she's my mate.

I smell her arousal and know even before I even slip my hand under her dress and beneath the panties she wears that I'll find her soaking wet.

My nostrils flare when my fingers meet the swollen flesh of her little pussy. I feel her pearly nub swollen and aching and flick my fingers across it.

She lets out a moan, her head falling back, exposing her neck to me.

I feel my fangs pressing against my gum line, threatening to descend, but I hold back. I'm not ready for that. Not yet. I want to taste the sweetness between her thighs first.

I drop to my knees in front of her like I'm getting ready to worship her, and I suppose I am. I just might put her on a pedestal and pay homage to this pussy day and night. Lick and suck and feast on it until neither of us can take any more. Pray to it.

I feel her little hands gripping onto my shoulders to keep herself from falling over. I hold the back of her thighs firmly as I rip her panties clean off of her and then press my nose right against her sweet little mound, inhaling deeply.

She smells like fucking heaven. "I may be damned," I snarl against her sensitive flesh, "but I've just found heaven. It's right here in between these sweet little thighs." I hear her whimper as my tongue snakes out to lave her from slit to clit.

She lets out a little gasp, her legs instinctively tightening against me, trying to close, but I hold them stubbornly open and begin to feast upon her in earnest.

"Sweeter than the finest cream, little one."

"Oh god," She mewls as her legs tremble beneath my hold. I release the back of one of her thighs to press a testing finger into her. She's so tight I can hardly get the digit in.

And Christ, my cock is leaking in envy, but as much as I'd love to thrust right up into her right now, I know that I have to prepare her for my swollen flesh that's way thicker than my fingers.

I insert a second and then a third finger slowly into her as I continue to suck and bat on her little clit.

She's gripping my shoulder so tightly I feel her claws digging into me. I relish in the feeling, probing deeper within her until I feel the thin barrier of her hymen, and then I retreat. I won't break that barrier until my cock is inside her. It's the only thing that's going to break her barrier.

She's panting and flushed all over. *My mate.* The possessive thought crashes through me, and I snarl against her while continuing to lap at her. I sense she's at the edge of orgasm, and I'm panting for it as much as her, dying to see her fall apart.

I increase the suction on her clit while swirling my tongue around it simultaneously.

And then she explodes with a loud, keening cry, and my god, she's glorious. Her cream is dripping down onto my face. I lap it up greedily like a cat licking up the sweetest milk. I groan as I feel a jet a precum shoot from my tip to stain the inside of my trousers.

She's still convulsing around my fingers when I finally can't take it anymore. I rip my trousers clean off me before I tear her dress from her body followed by her panties, leaving her completely naked before me. She's a work of art, perfectly sculpted, and I want to run my palms all over her naked skin.

I scoop her up in my arms and taste the sweet cherries of her nipples, sucking on them as I carry her over to her bed. She's arching up into me, offering her breasts to me. Another surge of male pride rushes through me at the evidence that she wants me just as much as I want her.

Still, I need to hear that confession before I make her totally mine. "Tell me you want this," I beg against her lips.

She stills beneath me, and I'm half afraid she's going to deny it. I rub my leaking cock against her thigh, unable to keep still, leaving a trail of moisture in my wake, the evidence of my own desire for her.

She moans at the contact before she finally admits softly, "Yes. Yes, Jasper. I want this."

A surge of lust so violent passes through me at her admission that I nearly stagger over. I fall upon her and kiss her deeply while I line my swollen staff up with her hole. "Fuck, Brenna," I grit out against her mouth as I start to push up into her.

My balls are so swollen that they ache, but she's plenty wet, and god knows my cock is providing plenty of lubrication as well. I'm leaking like a sieve.

I slip into her slowly, feeling the tight give of her flesh opening up to my intrusion. My chest is getting tighter with each torturous inch I push into her. She's so motherfucking tight I can't breathe.

I finally reach the barrier of her innocence. Knowing that the moment is upon us has me almost feral with need. I grab her throat in my hands, taking care to be as gentle as possible so I don't hurt her, but forcing her to meet my eyes. I want to see the moment I make her mine. I *need* to see that change in her eyes as she goes from innocent to woman.

"Look at me, sweet little bird," I command her.

Her sapphire blue eyes are glimmering up at me more beautifully than the most precious gemstone.

I taste her lips gently before I prompt her to look at me again. "Keep your eyes on me. Don't take them off me for a second."

For once, she obeys me without argument, and the absolute trust I see in her eyes is staggering.

The weight of responsibility settles on my shoulders. She's mine, and I'm going to take care of her forever. Give her pleasure, be her companion, her rock, anything she needs.

I finally rear back and thrust up into her deeply, breaking through her innocence.

She lets out a scream while I let out a guttural moan. "Mine!" I roar as I seat myself totally within her, my eyes rolling back in my head as I struggle not to come immediately.

Her arms wrap around me, her fingernails digging into my back and drawing blood, but I don't give a fuck. I'm shaking with the effort it takes not to move immediately. Instead, I hold myself still, letting her adjust to me while I suck on her sweet little nipples and kiss all along her collarbone up to her lips, soothing her. "It's okay, baby. Look at you with my big cock inside you. Took it so good. You did so good, honey."

I'm drowning her in praise, and I mean every motherfucking word. She's perfect. Perfect for me.

When I can't take it anymore, I do a testing probe. She moans, and I feel the muscles of her cunt tightening around me.

I groan at my own pleasure at the sensation. Christ, I'm not going to make it ten pumps with her milking me like this.

I grit my teeth and begin pumping into her slowly, focusing on not spilling too soon. She feels too motherfucking good and I'm not ready for this to be over yet.

I begin picking up the pace as all my instincts take over and I can hold back no longer. She wraps her little arms and legs around me.

"That's right baby. Hang on to me. I've got you," I rasp in her ear as I continue to rut into her more forcefully than I know I should for her first time, but fuck if I can stop.

She's moaning and whimpering and mewling in my ear, and my god if those sounds aren't an aphrodisiac all their own. I feel my balls drawing up and a tingle at the base of my spine. I know I'm close.

I feel the first fluttering of her pussy around me as I continue to ram up into her. "I need you to come for me, Brenna. Come all over your mate's dick with that sweet sugar, baby." I encourage her, continuing to spew filth in her ear, unable to control myself.

I finally feel her fall apart on me. Her back arches as she lets out a keening cry.

"Fuck!" I roar as her orgasm triggers my own release. I feel my seed ripping violently from my balls and shooting up my stalk to dump inside her hot channel.

"Fuck!" I roar again before screaming her name. My mouth falls upon her neck, and I bite down mindlessly, not even totally aware of what I'm doing until the sweet taste of her blood hits my tongue.

I drink her in greedily as I continue to pump everything I have into her. She's flowing into me while I'm flowing into her, and the sensation is so heady that I almost pass out.

"Jaspar!" she screams my name, and I finally manage to pull back from her, not wanting to drain her completely of her life

I gaze down at her, my eyes widening. Her eyes are going from sapphire to golden. A mixture of panic and fascination floods me as I watch the change overtaking her. She looks the same yet even more beautiful than before, if that's even possible.

"What?" she questions at my stupefied look, and I see the sharp points of her incisors lengthening. Her eyes widen as she no doubt feels what's happening to her now.

My brow furrows. I'm just as confused as she is. I didn't feed her any of my blood. There's no reason for her to be changing like this. What's more is she doesn't seem to be in any sort of pain, and pain is definitely typical of the change from human to vampire.

"Jasper," she whines. Her breathing ticks up, and her wild eyes look up at me.

I see them hone in on my neck, and somehow I instinctively know what she needs.

I offer my neck down to her. She takes it

without preamble. I feel the sting of the bite before I'm hit with a euphoric rush of pleasure that rivals that of when I had my own fangs sunk into the side of her neck.

She drinks from me deeply, and I come again as I share my lifeforce with her.

I'm coming so much that it's dripping out the sides of her pussy, making a sticky mess between our thighs and on the bed. My eyes roll back in my head. I've never come so much in my entire life.

She finally stops drinking from me and flops back down on the bed, her lips glistening red with my blood.

I lean down to kiss her, tasting my blood on her lips, licking her clean.

"How is this possible?" she asks.

I contemplate everything, just as puzzled as she is when it suddenly clicks within me.

"You said the prophecy said you had to kiss a vampire?" I ask her. "What exactly did the prophecy say?"

Brenna's eyes search mine curiously before she speaks.

"Seek the vampire's kiss or your power you'll

miss," she tells me, speaking slowly as she thinks it over herself.

I let out a little chuckle as it all makes sense now.

"Vampire's kiss is another name for the bite of a vampire, little bird. Our bite has been known as a kiss for centuries now."

Brenna blinks up at me as comprehension dawns on her face. "So, all this time I thought I had to kiss a vampire, all I needed was to be bitten by one."

"No," I growl down at her. "You better be glad you weren't bitten by any other vampire." The thought makes every muscle in my body tense up.

She strokes her hands over my arms, soothing me now. "I wouldn't want to be bitten by anyone but you either," she placates me.

"Good," I tell her, "because I will rip out the heart of anyone who even tries to."

She grins up at me before she rolls her eyes. "You're so insane."

"About my mate, yes," I tell her seriously.

Her eyes go wide again as she considers something new. "So my power is that I'm really a vampiress."

"It make sense," I tell her. "I was drawn to you from the moment I first saw you. I knew then you were my mate, but the only thing that didn't make sense was that you were a human."

"But I'm not anymore," she murmurs.

"No," I confirm. "Now, you're mine, my little vampires."

I nuzzle her cheek. "Do you realize you'd have found this out a lot sooner if you hadn't fought me so hard?" I point out to her with a raised eyebrow.

"Hey," she huffs out. "You kidnapped me. What was I supposed to do? Just fall into your arms."

"Exactly," I tell her with a huge smile, showing her my fangs.

"Insufferable vampire," she mumbles before she finally quirks her ruby red lips up into a little smile, wrapping her arms around my neck. "Well, I'm in them now," she concedes.

I brush her hair back from her face tenderly. My mate. My other half. My heart swells within me.

"Indeed you are, little bird, and right here is where you'll stay. Forever."

THE END

Want more books by Kenzie Skye?

Visit Kenzie Skye's website at www.
authorkenzieskye.com.